This Ladybird Book belongs to:

WELL DONE!

_____

_____

_____

_____

All children
have a great ambition …
to read by themselves.

Through traditional and popular stories, each title
in the **Read It Yourself** series introduces children to
the most commonly used words in the English
language (*Key Words*), plus additional words
necessary to tell the story.
The additional words appearing in this book are
listed below.

Dorothy, cyclone, picked, land,
witch, killing, wicked, didn't, shoes, magic,
Emerald, city, Oz, wizard, scarecrow,
brains, tin, woodman, heart, lion,
courage, spectacles, sends, monkeys,
goodbye, kill, thanked, working,
threw, dropped, wanted, melted

A catalogue record for this book is available
from the British Library

Published by Ladybird Books Ltd Loughborough Leicestershire UK
Ladybird Books Inc Auburn Maine 04210 USA

© LADYBIRD BOOKS LTD 1993
LADYBIRD and the device of a Ladybird are trademarks of Ladybird Books Ltd

The Wizard of Oz

adapted by Fran Hunia
from the original story by L F Baum
illustrated by Brian Price Thomas

Dorothy was at home
on the farm,
playing with her little dog.
She saw a cyclone coming,
so she picked up her little dog
and took him into the house.

The cyclone came.
It picked up Dorothy's house
and took it away.

The house came down
in a strange land.
A good witch came
to see Dorothy.
She thanked her
for killing the wicked witch.

"What wicked witch?"
asked Dorothy.
"I didn't kill a witch!"

Dorothy saw that
her house had landed
on the wicked witch.
She could see
the witch's shoes.

"You can have
the shoes," said
the good witch.
"They are magic."

Dorothy thanked her
and put on the shoes.

"I want to go home," said Dorothy.
"Can you help me, please?"

"You have to go
to the Emerald City
and ask the Wizard of Oz,"
said the good witch.

Dorothy and her little dog
walked on.

Soon they saw a scarecrow.
"Where are you going?"
asked the scarecrow.

"We are going
to the Emerald City to see Oz,"
said Dorothy.

"Can I come?"
asked the scarecrow.
"I want to ask Oz
to give me some brains."

Dorothy, her dog
and the scarecrow went on.
Soon they saw a tin woodman.

"Where are you going?"
asked the tin woodman.

"We are going
to the Emerald City to see Oz,"
said Dorothy.

"Can I go with you?"
asked the tin woodman.
"I want to ask Oz
to give me a heart."

"Come on, then," said Dorothy.

They all went on.
Soon they saw a lion.

"Where are you going?"
asked the lion.

"We are going
to the Emerald City
to see Oz," said Dorothy.

"Can I come with you?"
asked the lion.
"I want to ask Oz
to give me some courage."

"Come on, then," said Dorothy.

They all went on.
Soon they came
to the Emerald City.
A man gave them
some green spectacles.

They put them on
and went into the city.
It was all green.

A green girl took
Dorothy
to see Oz.

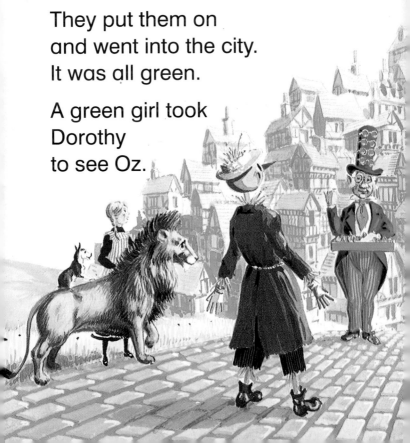

"Where did you get
the magic shoes?" Oz asked.

"My house killed
the wicked witch," said Dorothy.

"And what do you want
from me?" asked the wizard.

"I want to go home, please,"
said Dorothy.

"You can do something for me,
and then I can help you," said Oz.

"What do you want me to do?"
asked Dorothy.

"There is one more
wicked witch in this land,"
said Oz. "I want you to kill her."

Dorothy was very sad.

The scarecrow went to see Oz.

"Please can you give me
some brains?" he asked.

"First you must kill
the wicked witch," said Oz.
"Then I will give you some brains."

The scarecrow went sadly away.

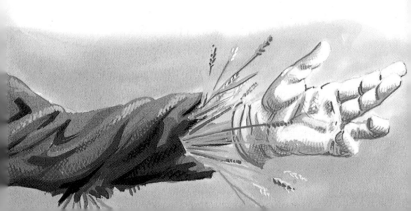

The tin woodman went
to see Oz.

"Please can you give me a heart?"
he asked.

"You will have to do something
for me," said Oz.
"Then I will give you a heart."

"What do you want me to do?"
asked the tin woodman.

"Kill the wicked witch," said Oz.

The tin woodman walked
sadly away.

The lion went to see Oz.

"Please can you give me
some courage?" he asked.

"You will have to kill the
wicked witch for me," said Oz.
"Then I will give you some
courage."
The lion went sadly away.

"We have to kill the wicked witch
or Oz won't help us,"
said the scarecrow.

They all went off to look
for the wicked witch.

The witch sent
some magic monkeys
to get Dorothy.
They took her back
to the witch.

The witch saw the magic shoes.
She wanted them.

"Give me the magic shoes,"
she said.

"No," said Dorothy.
"They are my shoes."

The witch made Dorothy
work for her.
She wanted Dorothy
to take her shoes off
so that she could have them.

When Dorothy was working
in the witch's house,
the witch took one of
her magic shoes.

Dorothy had some water.
She threw it at the witch,
and the witch dropped the shoe
and melted away.

Dorothy went to look
for the scarecrow,
the tin woodman,
and the lion.

"I have killed the witch,"
she said.
"We can go and see Oz,
and he can give us
all the things we want."

They all went to the Emerald City.
The scarecrow went to see Oz.

"We have killed
the wicked witch," he said.

Oz made some brains
and gave them to the scarecrow.
He gave the tin woodman a heart
and the lion some courage.

They were all very pleased.

"Please send me home,"
Dorothy said to Oz.

"I can't," said Oz sadly.
"I'm not a wizard at all.
I can't make magic."

"What can I do?" asked Dorothy.

"There is one more good witch,"
he said. "Go and see her.
She will help you."

Dorothy, her dog, the scarecrow,
the tin woodman, and the lion
all went off to see the good witch.

"What can I do for you?"
asked the good witch.

"I want to go home,"
said Dorothy. "Can you
help me, please?"

The good witch looked
at Dorothy's shoes.

"You have magic shoes,"
she said. "They will take you
home. All you have to do
is ask them."

Dorothy thanked the good witch.
She said goodbye
to the scarecrow,
the tin woodman, and the lion.
Then she picked up her little dog.

"Magic shoes,
please take me home," she said.

And soon she was at home
on the farm.

LADYBIRD
READING SCHEMES

Read It Yourself links with all Ladybird reading schemes and can be used with any other method of learning to read.

Say the Sounds

Ladybird's **Say the Sounds** graded reading scheme is a *phonics* scheme. It teaches children the sounds of individual letters and letter combinations, enabling them to tackle new words by building them up as a blend of smaller units.

There are 8 titles in this scheme:

1 **Rocket to the jungle**   5 **Humpty Dumpty and the robots**
2 **Frog and the lollipops**   6 **Flying saucer**
3 **The go-cart race**   7 **Dinosaur rescue**
4 **Pirate's treasure**   8 **The accident**

Support material available: Practice Books, Double Cassette pack, Flash Cards